Phonics

The Sand Goat

Sue Graves

W
FRANKLIN WATTS

First published in 2011 by
Franklin Watts
338 Euston Road
London NW1 3BH

Franklin Watts Australia
Level 17/207 Kent Street
Sydney NSW 2000

Text and illustration © Franklin Watts 2011

A CIP catalogue record for this book is
available from the British Library.

ISBN: 978 1 4451 0430 0 (hbk)
ISBN: 978 1 4451 0443 0 (pbk)

Illustrations by Artful Doodlers Ltd.
Art Director: Jonathan Hair
Series Editor: Jackie Hamley
Series Designer: Matthew Lilly

Printed in China

Franklin Watts is a division of
Hachette Children's Books,
an Hachette UK company.

www.hachette.co.uk

Level 1 50 words
Concentrating on CVC words plus and, the, to

Level 2 70 words
Concentrating on double letter sounds and new letter
sounds (ck, ff, ll, ss, j, v, w, x, y, z, zz) plus no, go, I

Level 3 100 words
Concentrating on new graphemes (qu, ch, sh, th, ng,
ai, ee, igh, oa, oo, ar, or, ur, ow, oi, ear, air, ure, er)
plus he, she, we, me, be, was, my, you, they, her, all

Level 4 150 words
Concentrating on adjacent consonants (CVCC/CCVC
words) plus said, so, have, like, some, come, were, there,
little, one, do, when, out, what

Polly and Eddy were at the beach with Mum and Dad.

They had lots of fun.
They ran in…

...and out of the sea.

They had a look at the big crabs and little crabs in the rock pools.

They put some sand in a bucket.
"Let's get lots of sand for a
sand pet!" said Polly.

"Yes!" said Eddy. "A sand
dog or cat. I like dogs
and cats."

"I like goats," said Polly.
"Let's do a sand goat!"

11

The sand goat was big!

But the goat was not good.
It stood on Mum's hat.

14

It ran off with Dad's socks.

It took Eddy's flip flop, too!
"What a bad goat!" said Eddy.

The sand goat got in a boat
and went out to sea.

"Next, let's do a little sand dog or cat," said Polly. "Sand goats are not good pets at all!"

Puzzle Time

Match the words that rhyme
to the pictures!

band

float

crab

sand

spent

drab

hand

goat

moat

slab

stand

went

tent

An w_.

crab – drab, slab   **goat** – float, moat

sand – band, hand, stand   **went** – spent, tent

Espresso Connections

This book may be used in conjunction with the Literacy area on Espresso to secure children's phonics learning. Here are some suggestions.

Word Machine

Encourage children to play the Word Machine Level 2. Demonstrate how the machine works, and then move on to the activities.

Ask children to find the correct beginnings. Then ask children to find the correct endings.

Check that children are able to hear the difference between the letter sounds as different words come up.

Praise plausible attempts, such as substituting the letter "k" for "c" when attempting to find the hard c sound.

Spot the Word

Choose a book from the Big Book selection to play Spot the Word.

Give children pieces of paper with the high frequency words **said, so, have, like, some, come, were, there, little, one, do, when, out** or **what**. (The class could be split, with groups of children looking for different words.)

Ask children to note down on the paper each time they have seen or heard the word they are looking for.

At the end of the book, children should count up how many times their target word has been used.

Go back through the book together and see whether they got it right.

Praise plausible attempts, for example "live" for "like" and take the opportunity to point out why these words are different.

You could replicate the activity with this phonics story.